HORRID HENRY'S
Mother's Day

HORRID HENRY'S
Mother's Day

Francesca Simon
Illustrated by Tony Ross

Orion
Children's Books

Horrid Henry's Mother's Day originally appeared in
Horrid Henry's Nightmare,
first published in
Great Britain in 2013
by Orion Children's Books
This edition published in Great Britain in 2015
by Orion Children's Books
a division of the Orion Publishing Group Ltd
Orion House
5 Upper St Martin's Lane
London WC2H 9EA
An Hachette UK company

1 3 5 7 9 10 8 6 4 2

Text © Francesca Simon 2013
Illustrations © Tony Ross 2015

ISBN 978 1 4440 1475 4

A catalogue record for this book is available from the British Library.

Printed in China

www.orionbooks.co.uk
www.horridhenry.co.uk

There are many more **Horrid Henry** books available.
For a complete list visit
www.horridhenry.co.uk
or
www.orionbooks.co.uk

Contents

Chapter 1

"What are you doing for
Mother's Day?" asked Perfect Peter.

Horrid Henry ignored him
and continued to read his
Screamin' Demon comic.

"I'm getting Mum flowers and
chocolates and making her breakfast
in bed," said Peter.

Horrid Henry scowled and slumped lower on the sofa.

"What presents are you getting her,
Henry?" asked Peter.

"None!" bellowed Horrid Henry.
"Now shut up and go away."

"Dad!" wailed Peter.
"Henry told me to shut up."

"Don't be horrid, Henry," said Dad.
"Or no TV tonight."

But Horrid Henry didn't care.
Mother's Day. Oh no. Not again.

Chapter 2

Horrid Henry hated Mother's Day.

Last year Peter gave Mum a giant hand–painted card covered in sparkles and glitter which had taken him weeks to make.

Last year Henry also made Mum
a card. Okay, so he'd folded over
a piece of paper and scrawled
"Happy Mother's Day" on it.

Was it *his* fault that the paper he'd
picked up off the floor had an advert
on the other side for a new kebab
shop opening down the road?

He'd been busy. He'd made her a card, hadn't he? Wasn't it the thought that counted?

But no. Mum was never satisfied.

Then Peter bought her a
massive bouquet of red roses so
Henry picked some tulips from
the garden and got told off.

It was so unfair.

Grrr. Aaaarrgh.

Why didn't they ever celebrate
Children's Day, that's what he
wanted to know. Then Mum
and Dad could serve him breakfast
in bed and buy him presents
and make him cards.

In fact, when Henry became King he'd make it the law that every day was Children's Day and Mother's Day and Father's Day would be banned.

Any parent trying to force their child to celebrate this horrible day would be buried headfirst in quicksand.

Naturally, Horrid Henry hadn't bought Mum a present. He'd been so busy watching TV and reading comics and playing on the computer and dragging his weary bones to school and back again that there just hadn't been any time.

And Mum and Dad were so mean
and horrid and gave him the puniest
amount of pocket money ever in the
history of the universe so how could
he be expected to buy a present
out of the few measly pence he had
rattling round his skeleton bank?

He couldn't and that was that.

If Mum and Dad wanted presents from him they should give him more cash.

Maybe Mum would forget about Mother's Day, thought Horrid Henry hopefully. She was getting old, after all, and didn't old people forget stuff?

"Well, boys," said Mum,
"I'm really looking forward to
Mother's Day tomorrow. I can't
wait to be pampered like a queen."

"You will be, Mum,"
said Perfect Peter. "I promise."

Chapter 3

Rats.

Rats.

Rats.

Rats.

 Rats.

Rats.

If only Peter weren't such a goody goody wormy worm toady toad.

Once again, Peter would put Henry to shame with his gifts

and his cards

and running to put a
cushion on Mum's chair

and making her
breakfast in bed

and . . .

Wait a minute.

Who said Peter had to outdo him this year? What if he, Henry, made Peter look horrid for once? What if, instead of ignoring Mother's Day, Henry made tomorrow a mother's day Mum would never forget?

What if he got Mum a fantastic card
and made her the best breakfast in
bed ever? In fact, if he bought a card,
it would be much better than
any home-made monstrosity
Peter had painted.

And, if he got up super early he could have Mum's breakfast all ready while Peter was still snoozing.

Ha! That would be the best trick ever. Henry couldn't wait to see Peter's shocked face when Peter brought up Mum's breakfast tray to find her already tucking into Henry's yummalicious treats.

"I've got a big surprise planned for you," said Perfect Peter.

"How exciting,"
said Mum, beaming.

"After all, you are the best mum in the world," said Peter.

"Thank you, Peter," said Mum.

Anything Peter could say
Henry could say better.

"Actually," said Henry,
"I think you're the best mum
in the universe."

Mum smiled. "Why thank you,
Henry," she said.

"You're the best mum who's ever lived," said Peter.

"You're the best mum who's ever lived and will ever live," said Henry.

Peter opened his mouth and then closed it. He couldn't think of anything to say to top that.

"Just wait till you see all the presents
I've got you, Mum," said Peter.
"How many do you have, Henry?"

"None of your business, worm,"
said Henry.

He glanced at the clock. Yikes.
He only had fifteen minutes before
the corner shop closed. Never mind.
It was sure to be filled with fabulous
Mother's Day cards and gifts.

"Be right back,"
shouted Horrid Henry.

Chapter 4

Henry stood in front of the Mother's Day card display. The shelf was empty. There wasn't a single Mother's Day card left.

How could there be no more cards?
His brilliant plan was ruined before
he'd even started.

He had to find a card.
If it just said, "Best wishes"
then he could write "Happy
Mother's Day" on the inside.

Yikes, every card in this
stupid shop cost so much.
Who knew cards were so expensive?

Wait.

There was a plastic box in
the corner filled with cards.
Any card 50 pence read the sign.
It was his lucky day!

Henry ran over and riffled
through them.

Shame about your Hernia

SORRY YOU'RE LEAVING

HAPPY 90TH BIRTHDAY

That'll do, thought Horrid Henry, grabbing the card. He'd cross out the *90th* and *birth* and write in *Mother's* instead.

She'll never notice, thought Horrid Henry.

Now, some presents.
What would Mum like?
Horrid Henry wandered
up the aisles.

Horrid Henry wandered
down the aisles.

He had three minutes left before
closing time to find the best
Mother's Day gifts ever.

What about a new toilet brush?
This pearly white one came with
a selection of cleaning supplies!
And matching toilet roll holder.
What a fantastic present.
Mum would be sure to love it.

On the other hand, it cost £4.99.
£4.99? Highway robbery. He'd
already spent 50p. And he had
comics to buy. He wasn't made of
money.

What about a DVD, *Beat Your Blubber*? Rats, even that was £1.99. If he bought it he'd have no money left for sweets this month. Besides, Mum didn't have much blubber to beat. Maybe *Growing Old Gracefully* would be better.

Aha. How about that book for 25p, *Hello Dentures*. The price was right, thought Horrid Henry, grabbing it. And he'd have cash left over for chocolate for him!

Hang on. What was Mum saying she needed just the other day? A new mop. Yes! She'd been moaning and moaning that the old one was falling apart. She'd love a new mop.

Actually, they were expensive. Rats. Why did everything cost so much? Wait. He was a genius. He'd just cut a rag into strips and then use a rubber band to attach them to the old mop handle.

Voila! A brand new mop. What mother wouldn't love such a great gift?

What a lucky mum she was,
thought Horrid Henry, as he strolled
home with his book and card.
Now all he had to do was to dream
up a few more fantastic gifts tonight,
and Mother's Day was sorted.

Peter was toast.

Chapter 5

Horrid Henry sat in his bedroom.
He'd made the mop.
What else could he give Mum?

Why not make her some coupons?
Genius. Another great gift for
Mother's Day, and, even better,
it wouldn't cost him a penny.
Horrid Henry got out some paper
and crayons, and wrote:

THIS MOTHERS DAY COUPON
IS GOOD FOR _____

What did mums like doing best of all? Cleaning up after their children! After all, Mum was lucky to have him for her child. She could have got someone really awful, like Weepy William, or Stuck-Up Steve.

In fact, any one else, really. Henry shuddered. Mum didn't know how lucky she was, having Henry for her son.

Horrid Henry filled in the coupon.

THIS MOTHERS DAY COUPON
IS GOOD FOR
Cleaning Henry's room

That was sure to make her happy.
In fact, why not be generous, and
give her a pack of ten?

There was a knock on his door.
"All ready for Mother's Day?"
asked Peter.

"Of course," said Henry smoothly.
"I've got Mum loads of presents and
I'm making her breakfast in bed."

Perfect Peter stood still.

"But that's *my* surprise," said Peter.
"*I'm* making her breakfast in bed."

Horrid Henry smiled.
"Tough," he said.

Peter glared at Henry.
Henry glared at Peter.

Ha, thought Horrid Henry.
He'd get up super early to make sure
he got Mum's breakfast ready first.
He'd do soft boiled eggs, toast, jam,
juice, tea – the works.

Tee hee Peter, thought
Horrid Henry.
If you snooze, you lose.

Chapter 6

Clink. Clink. Clunk. Clunk.

Horrid Henry opened one eye.
It was still dark outside. Who could
be moving about the kitchen making
so much noise so early?

Then Horrid Henry sat up. Peter!
That little ratty toad.
He'd got up early to beat Henry.
Well, not so fast.
Henry bolted out of bed and
dashed into the kitchen.

There was Peter bustling around, getting out napkins and cutlery on a tray decorated with a red rose.

"Whatcha doin', worm?"

"Making Mum her Mother's Day breakfast in bed," said Peter, placing two pieces of toast in the toaster.

"Glad someone is,"
said Henry, yawning.

Peter paused.
"Aren't you making her breakfast,
Henry?" asked Peter.

"Nah," said Henry. "You go ahead."

Then Henry cocked his head and
went to the door.
"Peter, Dad's calling you."

"I didn't hear anything," said Peter.

"Okay, I'll go," said Henry.

"He said it was about
Mother's Day..."

Peter shot out of the kitchen
and dashed upstairs.

Chapter 7

Henry nipped to the toaster.

 Zip!

Peter's toast was out and in the bin.

Pop!

Horrid Henry put in four pieces of toast, then stood guard.

Perfect Peter dashed back into
the kitchen.
"Dad didn't call me," said Peter.
"He was asleep."

"Yeah he did," said Henry.

"No he – where's the toast I was
making Mum?" said Peter.

Henry ignored him.

"Where's Mum's toast?" said Peter.

"What toast?" said Henry.

"You took my toast out of the toaster!"

"Didn't."

"Did."

"Didn't."

"Liar."

"Liar."

Slap!

Slap!

"Mum!" screamed Henry and Peter.

"Henry slapped me," yelled Peter.

"Peter slapped me first,"
yelled Henry.

"Didn't!"

"Did!"

"Liar!"

"Liar!"

Dad stumbled
in just as
Henry pulled
Peter's hair.
Peter started
screaming.

68

"Henry! Leave your brother alone," he shouted. "It's Mother's Day."

"I'm making her breakfast in bed, and then Peter came in and tried to steal my toast," said Henry.

Peter gasped.
"I was making her toast first," he wailed. "Henry's lying."

Dad sighed.
"Why don't you *both* make her
breakfast in bed?" he said, yawning
and stumbling back upstairs.

Henry looked at Peter.
Peter looked at Henry.

"Sure, Dad," said Horrid Henry.

Henry raced to the toaster,
yanked out the toast and threw it
on a red tray. No time for a plate.
Or butter. Now for the eggs.
Peter snatched the jam and put it on
his tray, then poured some juice
and got out the cereal.

Oh no. Peter was getting ahead of him! He'd be first upstairs with his breakfast, and all Henry's hard work would be for nothing.

Henry dashed to the fridge, snatched two eggs and flung them into egg cups. No time to soft boil them. Anyway, they'd just be a bit runnier than normal, right?

Henry frantically poured orange
juice into a glass and ran to the
door with his tray. Forget the tea.
Peter pounded after him,
clutching his breakfast tray.

Henry shoved his tray in front
of Peter, blocking him,
then galloped up the stairs.

Victory!

"Happy Mother's Day,"
screamed Horrid Henry, bursting
into Mum and Dad's bedroom.

"Happy Mother's Day,"
screamed Perfect Peter, jostling
Henry as he burst into the room.

"Huunhn," grunted Mum.

Henry tried to shove Peter
out of the way with his tray.

Peter tried to shove Henry
out of the way with his tray.

Slosh!

Juice went all over Henry's tray
and spilled over Mum.

Cereal went all over Peter's tray
and spilled over Mum.

Smash!

Crash!

Mum was covered in runny raw egg,
broken shells, juice and cereal.
"Yum," she said faintly.

"Don't worry, Mum,"
yelled Horrid Henry. "I've got just
the perfect present to mop you up!"

What are you going to read next?

Have more adventures with Horrid Henry,

or save the day with Anthony Ant!

Become a superhero with Monstar,

float off to sea with Algy,